THE MAGICAL ADVENTURES OF *Cpt'n Blackheart*

by

Pam Vince

Paperback ISBN 978-1984302717

To our much loved and beautiful grandchildren
Daniel, Daisy and Harley.

May your adventures be many.

A big thank you to my lovely husband Ric for his many hours of encouragement, his fantastic illustrations, his editing of script and his guidance in the life of a pirate.

Love you Cpt'n.

I also thank my family and friends who sat and listened to my stories again and again, with only words of encouragement.

Please sign the Pirate Code on the dotted line to be part of

Cpt'n Blackheart's Magical Crew.

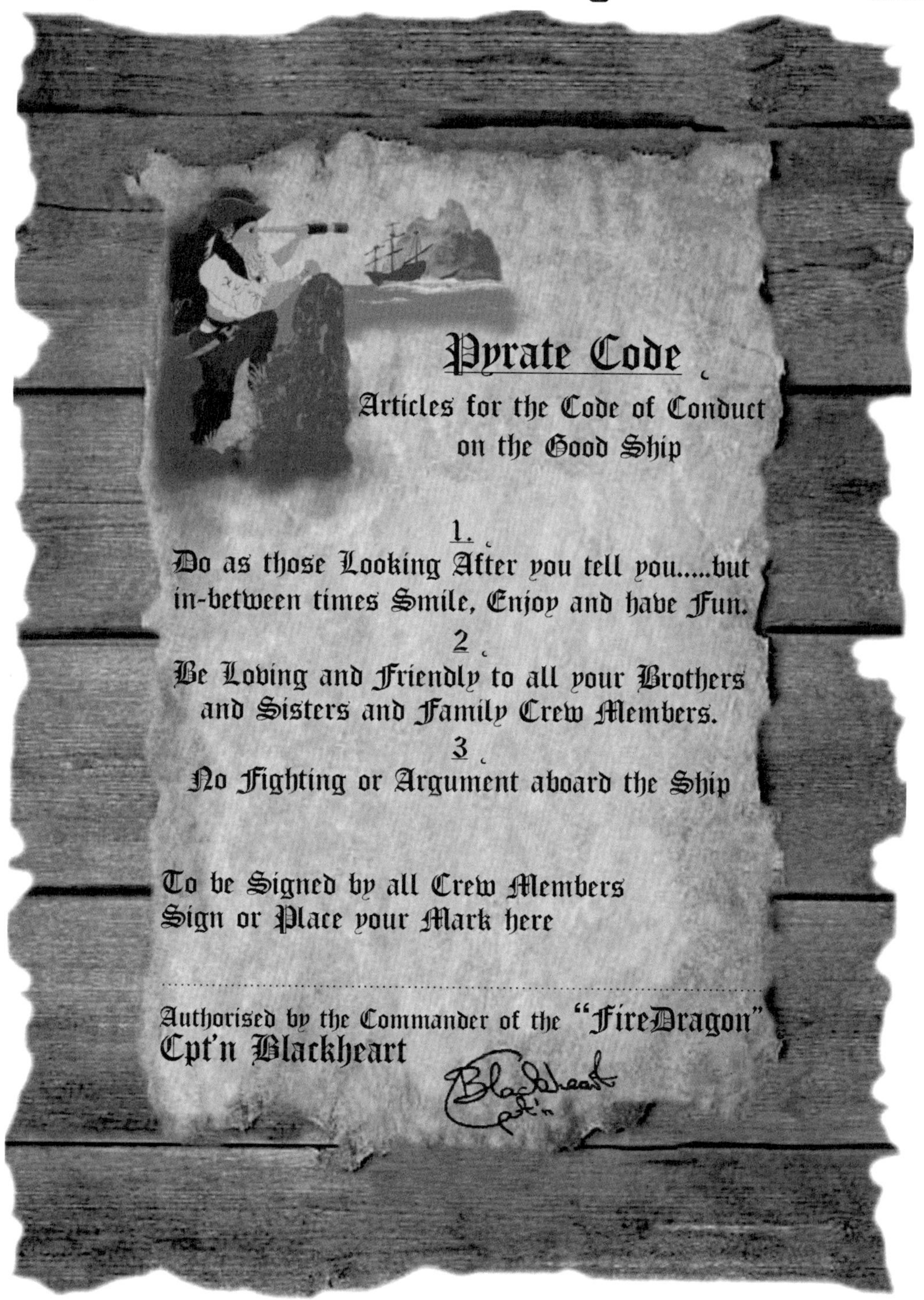

Pyrate Code

Articles for the Code of Conduct on the Good Ship

1.

Do as those Looking After you tell you.....but in-between times Smile, Enjoy and have Fun.

2.

Be Loving and Friendly to all your Brothers and Sisters and Family Crew Members.

3.

No Fighting or Argument aboard the Ship

To be Signed by all Crew Members
Sign or Place your Mark here

....

Authorised by the Commander of the "FireDragon"
Cpt'n Blackheart

James and Matt

You see, it's never too late!!!!!

Darcy the Mermaid upon a rocky outcrop close to where Cpt'n Blackheart lives.

Contents

Illustrations

Front Cover and Contents

Captain Blackheart outside his secret cave overlooking his ship "the FireDragon" waving to Darcy the Mermaid.

Back Cover

Captain Blackheart waving to Darcy the Mermaid, his ship the "Fire Dragon" in the background, George the Octopus having words with Cpt'n Blackheart, the Higeldies taking a swim and Martha and Eddy, the Seagulls, diving down to see the Captain.

Pirate Code

Sign the Pirate Code to become part of Captain Blackheart's Magical Crew aboard his Pirate Ship the "FireDragon". Please sign, write your name or put your mark upon the dotted line to become part of the crew.

1. Cpt'n Blackheart

Captain Blackheart outside his secret cave overlooking his ship the "FireDragon" and looking through his spyglass (Telescope) checking to see that the coast is clear for him to leave.

2. Darcy the Mermaid

1. Cpt'n Blackheart waving to Darcy the Mermaid.
2. Seagulls flying around in panic looking for Cpt'n Blackheart.
3. Cpt'n Blackheart stopped to sit down on a rock to look up at the seagulls.
4. Martha the seagull sees the Captain and flies down to him fast.
5. Cpt'n, Cpt'n, Cpt'n the seagulls all squark together.
6. Sprat the Crab quickly buries himself in the sand and then peeps out to see if the coast is clear.
7. Cpt'n Blackheart leaps into his canoe and follows the seagulls.

8. A few little crabs holding on to one another trying desperately to pull Darcy up onto the rocks.
9. Darcy said she thought everything in the sea was her friend.
10. The Seagulls started mimicking the Captain.
11. Seagulls flying off to fetch the Medicine man.
12. The seagulls flew off chanting "fetch the medicine man, fetch the medicine man".
13. Captain Blackheart scooped Darcy up and placing her carefully into his canoe, he paddled off as if his life depended upon it as Darcy's long hair blew wildly in the wind
14. The Medicine man running towards the Captain and Darcy the Mermaid, across the rocks and sand as fast as he could.
15. It looked as if half the crabs from the ocean had gathered around and started snapping their pincers in approval
16. Captain Blackheart took out a little bottle and held it gently against Darcy's cheek.

17. Darcy thanked the Captain and the medicine man and then with a flick of her tail she was gone.
18. "Did you see what bit Darcy?" the Captain first asks some little crabs. Lucas a very big Spiny Spider Crab speaks first.
19. George the octopus puts a tentacle around the Captains shoulder as a friendly gesture.
20. "She's here, she's here" called a very excited turtle, "I've found Mother shark".
21. Mother shark, whose name is Pippa, quickly swims towards the Captain with Rosie and Robin, the Higeldies, fast in pursuit.
22. Pippa, the mother shark with her baby Rocko having a big nudge hug, which is the only way sharks know how to hug.
23. There on a rock near by Darcy sat, tail partly submerged in the sea and waving over to Pippa and Rocko.
24. The Higeldies and other fish.
25. Captain Blackheart outside his magical cave.
26. More Fish......friends of Cpt'n Blackheart.

Cpt'n Blackheart

Captain Blackheart outside his secret cave overlooking his ship the "FireDragon" and looking through his spyglass (Telescope) checking to see that the coast is clear for him to leave.

THE REAL LIFE

Cpt'n Blackheart

Cpt'n Blackheart, upon who these short stories are based, is in fact a real life Pirate who can be seen down upon the waterfront and streets of Brixham, a quaint old fishing village found upon the southern shore of Torbay, South Devon.

"Cpt'n Blackheart o' Brixham" to give him his full title or as many a local call him "The Brixham Pirate", is a very friendly character, very approachable, and with a fine knowledge of his trade can tell you all about pirates and piracy, how they lived, life aboard a ship and much much more.

Take time out when you are in the area to search him out and speak to him, I'm sure you will not be disappointed.

Cpt'n Blackheart

Cpt'n Blackheart is over 500 years old, cursed by Davey Jones, for his soul to live for ever and ever………

but thanks to a Sorceress who he met on his journeys and made friends with, the Captain now lives a very magical life.

Returning to the little shanty town on the South Devon coast from where he was born, Cpt'n Blackheart now lives between a magical secret cave, of which only a few people know about and his pirate ship the 'Fire Dragon' which now nestles in a little sheltered bay where no landlubbers can reach from land.

The term 'Landlubbers' or 'Lubbers', as the word is so often shortened to, was a word used by seamen in the olden days for those people who never went out to sea.

Cpt'n Blackheart has a very big bushy beard, this he says keeps him warm in the winter. He has also many friends, some who live in the town near-by and some over the sea and faraway but they always come back to visit the Captain and are always very excited to help him in his adventures

Here is the first of the short stories about the Cpt'n Blackheart and his friends of which there are many many more to come.

I hope you enjoy them all and when you visit the quaint little harbour town of Brixham on the South Devon shores, be sure to keep a look out for 'Cpt'n Blackheart', the man the locals call the "Brixham Pirate" or "The Blackheart o' Brixham".

and be sure to say -

"Ahoy there Cpt'n",

in which case he will return by saying,

"Ahoy ter 'ee me 'earty"

and give you a good luck high five.

Cpt'n Blackheart and Darcy the Mermaid

Darcy the Mermaid upon a rocky outcrop close to where Cpt'n Blackheart lives.

Main Characters in the Story
Darcy the Mermaid

DARCY –

A young Mermaid who has become very good friends with the Captain and who cares for the animal life below water. She sometimes helps to guide the Captain's ship "FireDragon" to safety when it becomes in danger.

MARTHA AND EDDIE –

Two Seagulls of the Herring Gull family, who often sit outside the Captain's cave when he's not on his ship. Years gone by the Captain rescued both of these Seagulls when they were caught in a very bad storm. He found them both laying injured and exhausted upon a beach so he took them back to his cave to look after them and get them better. They are both very trusted friends of the Captain within his magical world.

George –

A very gentle but humorous Octopus who being one of the Captains oldest friends, has followed the Captain far and wide across the oceans, always very keen to help him. Being able to magically expand his size to that of a Kraken, the Captain finds him a very valuable friend.

Rosie and Robin –

Two very colourful fish from a special group of fish called the Higeldies, an underwater species conjured up by Captain Blackheart's Sorceress to act as the Captain's eyes and ears beneath the seas.

Lucas –

A large Spiny Spider Crab who is a knowledge of all that goes on. Always willing to help the Captain any way he can.

Sprat –

A very friendly little shore crab who will put himself out to help just about anyone, especially the Captain.

Pippa –

A female Shark, mother to Rocko.

Rocko –

A baby Shark, son to Pippa.

Darcy the Mermaid

As Cpt'n Blackheart walked along the beach he sensed something strange was going on above him.

Looking up, he could see the seagulls flying in a panic and the noise they were making, squawking so loudly, it sounded quite scary.

What could have done this to them? Why were they flying in such a way he thought to himself.

All of a sudden the seagulls saw Captain Blackheart, who, having seen them flying around in circles above him, making him feel quite dizzy, stopped to sit down on a big rock near by to look up at them.

The Captain had a very special connection with all animals, magic you might say, where animals could talk to the Captain and let him know exactly what was going on out at sea, far away on land or even just on his own doorstep.

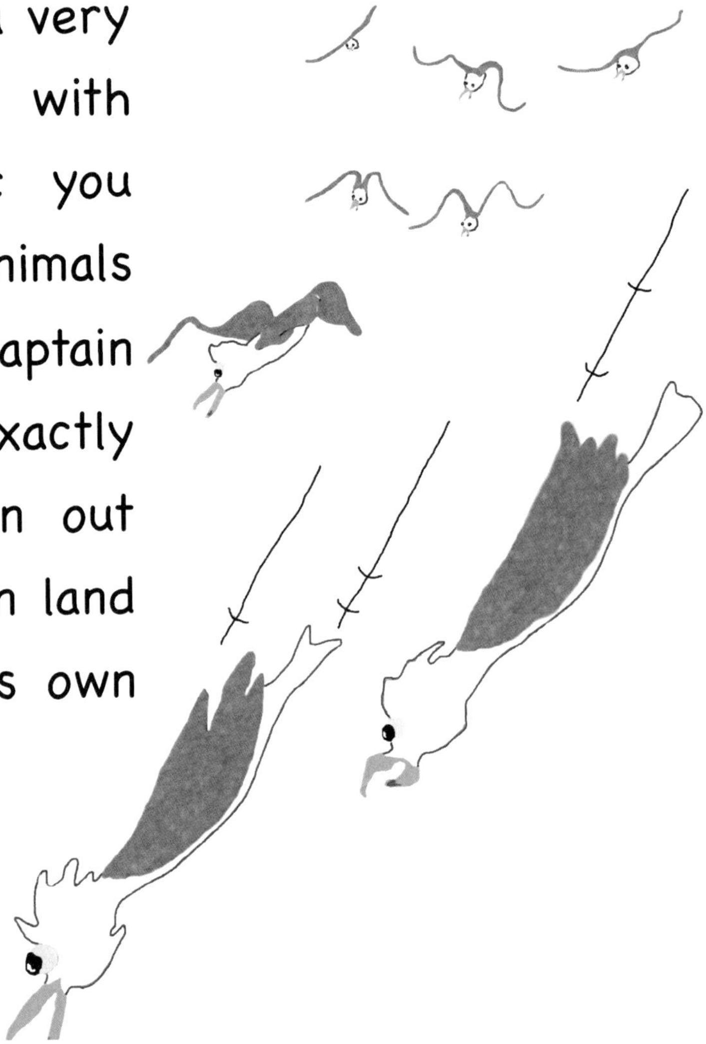

Martha, one of the seagulls, sees the Captain first and flies down to him as fast as she can. Eddie, another seagull, just can't keep up with her as she's flying so fast.
Before long all the seagulls are following Martha.

"Cpt'n, Cpt'n Cpt'n" they all squawk together, making such a noise the Captain can't even hear himself think!

"Wait a minute, wait a minute" said the Captain "I can't understand a word of what you are trying to tell me, Martha, what is it, tell me what's going on".

"Captain, it's Darcy the mermaid she's in trouble" cried Martha!

"What!! Where?" shouts the Captain as he jumps up and dashes across the sand.

Leaping up over the rocks, he just misses Sprat the crab,

who quickly buries himself in the sand, peeping out to see if the coast is clear.

"Follow us, follow us" the seagulls screeched, in such a way that only the Captain could understand them. Leaping into his canoe he follows the seagulls across the ocean.

In the distance he could see something floundering about in the sea, it was Darcy the mermaid desperately trying to hang on to a rock. There were a few little crabs who seemed to be standing in a group holding on to one another trying desperately to pull Darcy up onto the rocks but with very little success.

Huffing and a puffing, they were all very grateful to see the Captain.

"Oh Darcy you're bleeding, what happened?" asked the Captain. Darcy could barely lift her head, she felt so weak,

"Oh Captain, you came, thank you. Captain, I thought everything in the sea was my friend but when I put my hand out to stroke a little fish, something bit me on my tail,

Oh Captain, it bit me so hard it really hurts me".

"Poor Darcy" the Captain thought, "she wouldn't even hurt a shrimp".

"I must find out who did this to you Darcy but first lets get you to my medicine man as quickly as possible".

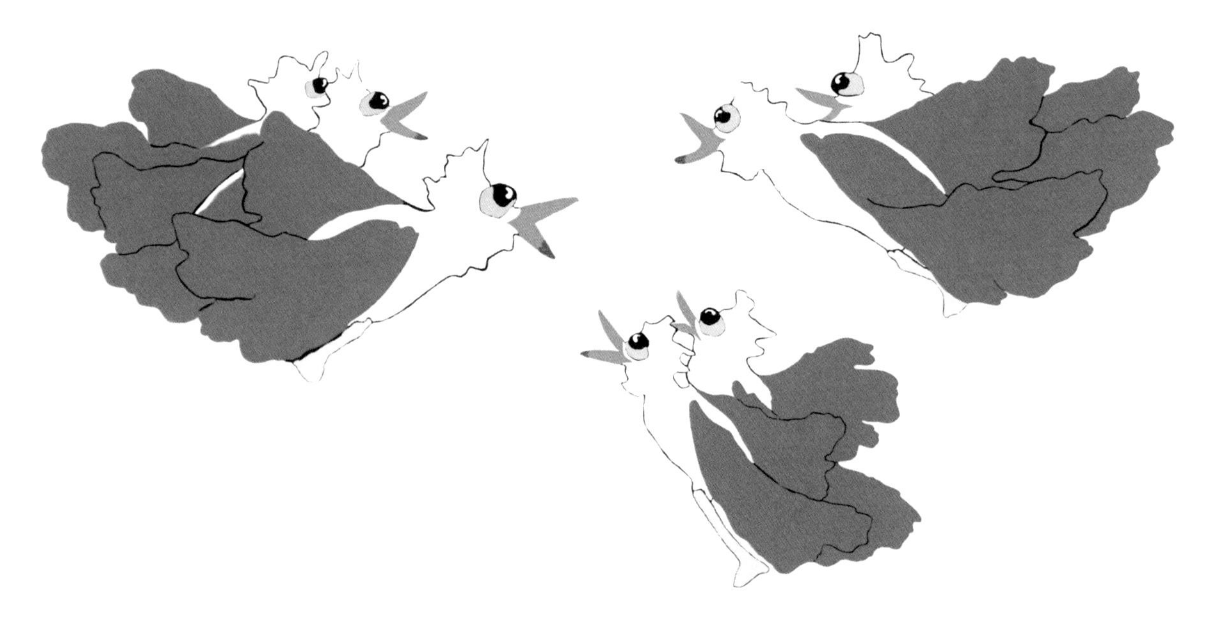

The seagulls started mimicking the Captain "as quickly as possible, as quickly as possible" they squawked.

"Yes that's right my friends, now fly off and fetch my medicine man and we'll meet him by the rocks on the beach".

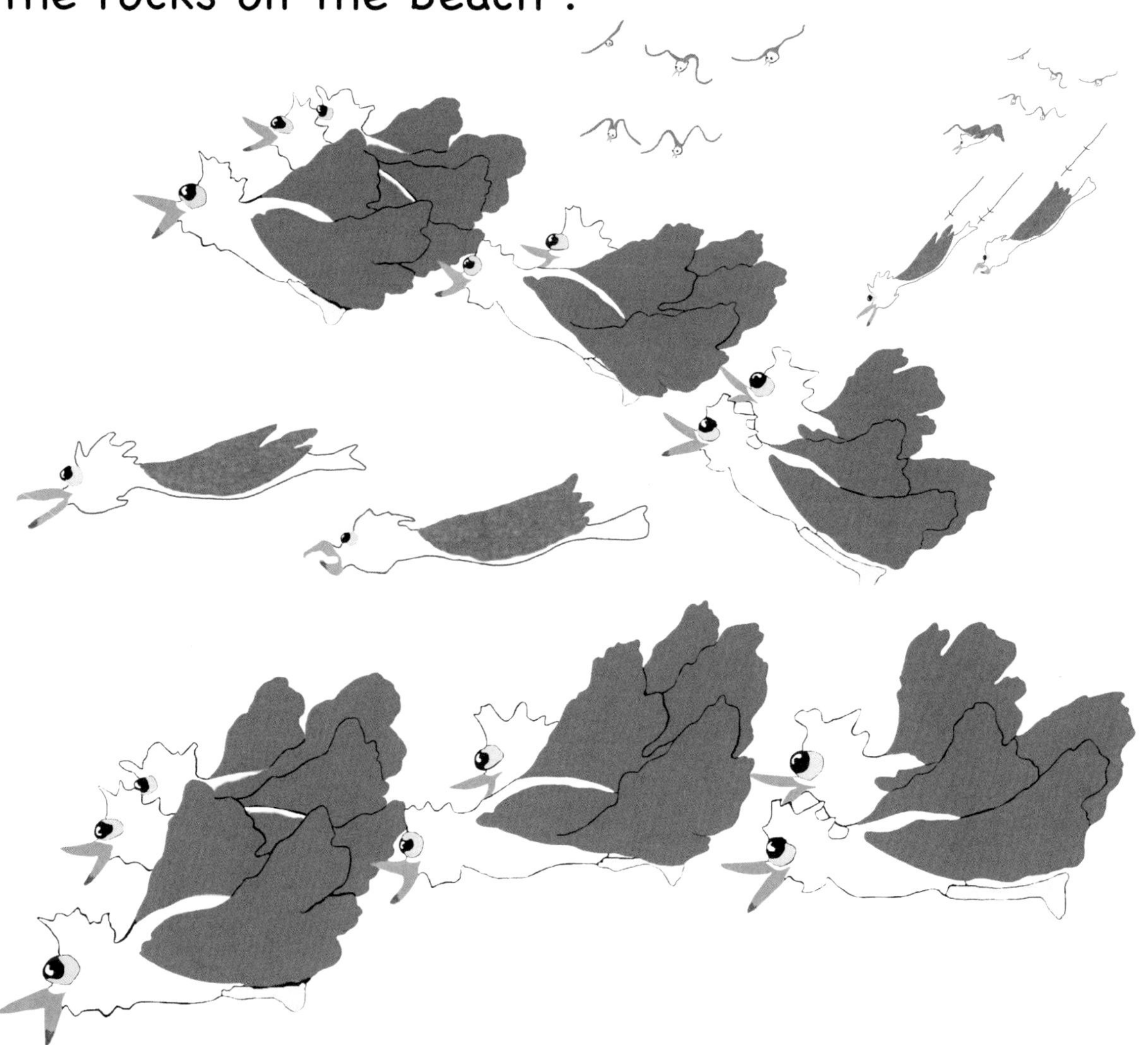

Without another word the seagulls flew off looking like a flying carpet and chanting as they flew "fetch the medicine man, fetch the medicine man".

Captain Blackheart scooped Darcy up and placing her carefully into his canoe, paddled off as if his life depended upon it.

In fact, he rowed that fast that Darcy's long hair blew wildly in the wind looking as if it had a mind of it's own, swirling and dancing around and around. Darcy clung onto both sides of the boat, her heart beating very fast.

The Captain was very determined to get Darcy to land as quickly as possible, just so his medicine man could start healing her before she lost much more blood.

As they got close to the shore, the Captain noticed his medicine man running towards them across the sand and over the rocks, his big black bag in his hand full of everything that he might need.

The Captain lifted Darcy out of the boat and gently placed her on the soft sand close to some rocks that he had been sat on only a short while earlier.

There was a cheering from what looked like half the crabs of the ocean, who having watched what was going on, decided to all gather around and started snapping their pincers in approval.

Darcy the little mermaid couldn't help tears from rolling down her face and knowing that mermaid tears had magical powers known only to the Captain, looked up at him and said

"Captain, please take my tears, I know you can use them and it's my way of saying thank you. Please take them before they dry up".

So Captain Blackheart, took out a little bottle from his pouch and holding it gently against Darcy's cheek, caught her tears one by one, drip, drip, drip, until his bottle was full.

"Thank you Darcy" said the Captain, "Thankin' 'ee kindly".

Whilst the Captain was doing this, the medicine man had been mending Darcy's tail and now she was fully recovered and ready to go back to sea.

"Just take care" says Cpt'n Blackheart "and remember, you can't touch just anything you like in the sea, somethings can be very dangerous as you've just found out, even poisonous but most things are usually OK, so go off & have fun, just be careful".

Darcy thanked the Captain and the medicine man and then with a flick of her tail, disappeared back off into the deep sea from where she had come.

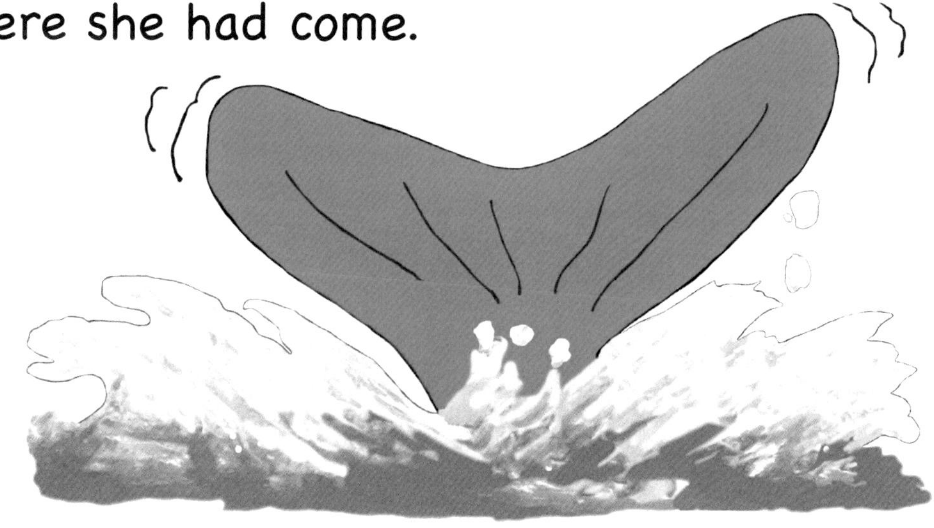

After the Captain and medicine man had a little chat, they parted company, the medicine man going back to his work aboard the ship and the Captain to find out some answers. If there was anything in the sea biting people and animals then he needed to know who & why.

"Did you see what bit Darcy?" the Captain first asks some little crabs who had been watching everything that had been going on. Lucas a very big Spiny Spider Crab speaks first

"Captain, I think it was a baby shark who was lost,

I think he was scared and bit Darcy out of fear, I don't think he meant to bite her but the little fish are trying to find out".

Oh look here's George the octopus, maybe he knows. George the octopus puts a tentacle around the Captains shoulder as a friendly gesture and says

"Well Captain, it's like this, It was a baby shark who had become separated from his Mother. He was really scared, he's never seen a hand before

and thought it was going to hurt him, he panicked and just did what came naturally. I've just been talking to him, he doesn't even know his name but he is very sorry for biting Darcy and just wants to find his Mother".

The Captain, turning towards the sea, starts chanting "Mother Shark, come find your baby, your poor lost baby, Mother shark come find your baby" his words are like magic as they bounce through the waters until the sea becomes alive with all the creatures looking for her.

"She's here, she's here" called a very excited turtle, "I've found Mother shark".

Sure enough, Mother shark, whose name is Pippa quickly swims towards the Captain, crying, "Oh you have found my baby, oh thank you, thank you. We were separated when some person threw their rubbish into the ocean, it hit me square in the face knocking me out and I sank to the bottom of the sea. If it wasn't for Rosie and Robin, the Higeldies (the Higeldies being a type of very colourful fish), I would still be there."

The Captain could see George the octopus beckoning to something in the sea with one of his tentacles and shouting out.

"It's the baby shark! Come on, come on don't be shy little one, your Mother's here, she's been very worried and she has been looking all over for you". So after a big nudge hug, which is the only way sharks know how to hug,

Pippa, the mother shark, told everyone that they'll be on their way now and so would they please say sorry to Darcy for both of them for what had happened.

There on a rock near by Darcy was sat, tail partly submerged in the sea and waving over to them.

"It's OK I forgive you, we gave each other a shock, it's OK".

So Pippa, the mother shark with her baby who's name is Rocko swished their tales and as if by magic, totally disappeared into the depths as fast as they had come.

"I hope this has taught everyone a lesson" said the Captain, "don't presume everything in the ocean is ok to touch, just be careful and stick together. Also remember, rubbish of any kind is not ok to throw in the ocean, not just because of pollution but also you may just hit someone on the head!!!"

"Good night creatures out at sea and on land, good night.

Oh! and seagulls before I forget, if you are up early enough, the fishing trawlers are going out to sea as soon as the sun rises.

I have had a word with all their skippers and they say that if you follow them, they'll give you all treats for helping little Darcy".

The seagulls made such a noise that the Captain had to put his hands over his ears.

"Yes, yes, good night, good night" shouted the Captain and off he wondered back to his magical cave until his next adventure.

Be a-seein' 'ee soon me hearties,

Be a-seein' 'ee soon

Made in the USA
Lexington, KY
15 April 2018